# THE TRIDENT SERIES

## A TRIDENT WEDDING

Book 9

Jaime Lewis

The Trident Series – A Trident Wedding
Copyright © 2021 by Jaime Lewis

ISBN: 978-1-952734-26-7

# TABLE OF CONTENTS

# CHAPTER ONE

Alex took the long path through the cemetery as she made her way toward the back where the memorial park for veterans was located. Many people might not consider a cemetery beautiful, but as she looked out at the rows upon rows of gravestones nestled beneath trees with blossoming flowers, it was like a landscape like no other. It was a garden of beautiful souls who had been laid to rest.

As she approached the stone bench, she drew in a deep breath. In front of her was a winter white gravestone with the American flag affixed to it waving in the gentle breeze. Inscribe were the words; always loved, never forgotten, forever missed.

She'd been coming to this spot since she was six years old, and it never got any easier. In fact, some visits were more difficult, such as today.

She bent over and brushed off the few leaves that had fallen from the tree above.

"Hey, daddy," she whispered over the lump of emotion that had taken up residence in her throat.

She inhaled again before closing her eyes. It had been a few weeks since she visited. Ever since she moved back to town, she had made the time to visit once a week. But because of her hectic schedule, it had been a few weeks since she last visited.

"I really wish you were here right now. I'm feeling a little lost and confused and don't really know who to talk to. I feel like everyone is moving on, and I'm stuck behind. I don't know, maybe I've stretched myself too thin by taking on so much, and I'm feeling out of sorts because of the stress of it all."

"You left me with a wonderful man who has raised me to be the woman I think you thought I'd grow into. Everyone always tells me how they see a lot of you in me. Every time I hear that it brings a smile to my face." She smiled. "It's funny that at times I can still hear your deep laughter."

"The Foundation is thriving. I should be hearing any day now if the expansion project in Coronado is going to move forward. I know there's been a lot of support for it. I wish you could be here to witness it all."

"Everyone is doing well," she smiled. "This will shock you—Tink found a woman. Though not the way he probably imagined meeting the woman meant for him. I guess that saying that *love hits you when you least expect it* is true."

"I know I've told you a lot about Ace. He is such a wonderful man, and I know that if you had the chance to meet him that you'd love him too. He's so much like you were—a badass with a heart full of love."

Her breath caught in her throat as she became overwhelmed with emotion.

"I love him with all my heart, and I know he loves me too." She paused. "But I'm starting to wonder if it's enough. I feel like at times that he and I aren't aligned, and we both have busy schedules, but…" her voice started to drift off. "I don't know; maybe it's just me feeling sorry for myself."

"I've been independent for most of my adulthood, but the last two years, I've leaned on him a lot. We're both doing wonderful things, but I wish we could just finalize our love for one another. I want to give him that part of me. I want to be his wife. I want to have a family."

"I don't want to be that person who walks away. I want to stand by his side because I'm so damn proud of him and what he stands for."

In reality, she didn't want to be her mom.

A breeze blew in, and she tilted her face up toward the sky and closed her eyes as the warm sunshine warmed her cheeks and dried her trail of tears.

In the distance, a bugle played taps. A sign that another soldier was being laid to rest.

She suddenly felt the presence of someone behind her. She looked over her shoulder and found Derek there. He was in his Type III uniform. She knew there were days during his lunch breaks that he would visit her dad.

2

The day her dad was killed, Derek not only lost a teammate, but he also lost his best friend.

She scooted over to make room for him, and he sat down.

"I guess you heard all that?" she said with a small smile as she wiped the tears from her eyes.

"I did." He took her hand and held it. It was comforting as they sat in silence for a few minutes.

"He loved you so much. You were the apple of his eye," he told her as he looked toward the gravestone.

She stared straight ahead because she knew that she would burst into tears if she looked at him.

"You know that Ace loves you too, right?"

She looked at him. "I know he does."

"I couldn't have asked for a better man to ask you to marry him." He snorted a small laugh. "Although, I still can't believe you're engaged to a SEAL."

She smiled, then shrugged her shoulders. "What can I say. He was persistent."

"He wanted something, and he went after it. And, you were right—your dad would have absolutely loved him." He patted her leg. "Have faith, sweetie. I'm sure things will all work out," he winked, and she noticed the slight twinkle in his eye.

*What was he up to?*

# CHAPTER TWO

Ace was running around Bayside feeling like a chicken with its head cut off. Arianna and Campbell both approached him.

"Ace, you need to chill," Arianna told him as she tried to hold back her laughter at seeing how flustered Ace was. It wasn't often the Lt. Commander, and SEAL team leader got in a tizzy.

For Ace, it wasn't a laughing matter. He ran his hand nervously through his thick black hair. How could he be chill when he was trying to pull off the biggest surprise for Alex? Everything had to be perfect.

"I can't. I'm a fucking wreck right now. I feel like something's going to fall through the cracks."

Campbell chuckled as she stood next to Arianna with her trusty clipboard in hand. "Ace, I'm telling you, everything is spot-on. The room, table settings, food, and you name it, are all just as how you requested it."

He took a deep breath and looked around the private room at Bayside. It looked stunning. He couldn't have asked for anything better. Campbell was damn good at her job. She was a creative genius when it came to party planning. He had snuck into Alex's wedding planning room at the house and had found a picture of a wedding rehearsal dinner that Alex had pulled from a magazine. He had given it to Campbell and told her to get the room to look as close as she could to the photograph. And damn if she hadn't nailed it. She had made the space even more special by adding a few personal touches around the room, such as photos of Ace and Alex over the last two years.

His eyes went to the one picture that sat at the front of the room on an easel. It was his all-time favorite picture of the two of them. It had been taken in Afghanistan—the place where they met and their journey together began. One of the guys had captured the intimate moment when they weren't looking.

He closed his eyes, remembering that evening. He and Alex had been walking back to their barracks when they stopped to witness the most stunning sunset he'd ever seen. Whoever took the picture had captured a

4

moment that they'd never be able to recreate. She had been looking up at him as he had been gazing into her eyes. They were both smiling, while behind them, the sky was layered in yellow, orange, red, and blue as the day transitioned into night.

"I remember that night." The voice behind him said and turned then smiled seeing Potter, his best friend standing there looking at the picture.

Ace smiled. "It was a sight to see."

Potter smirked. "It looks like it."

More of their friends and family began to file in.

After giving in to Campbell and Arianna and understanding that he had done all he could do, he walked over to everyone to greet them.

"What in the hell is all of this about?" Stitch asked as he scanned the room.

Others were making comments, especially the ladies. They were fawning all over the creativity that Campbell had outdone herself with.

Ace grabbed a beer from the bar and took a swig.

"Well, now that everyone is here. I would like to officially welcome you to Alex and mine's joint bachelor/bachelorette party."

He hid his smile when he heard all the gasps and saw the surprised expressions on everyone's faces, except for Derek, who was aware of Ace's plans. Ace had made sure to include Derek in all of the planning because specific components in both the ceremony and reception would be a tribute to Alex's dad.

Skittles was the first one to say something. "How did you guys manage to keep this a secret?"

Ace grinned. "Alex doesn't know yet. This a surprise for her."

"Holy shit. I'm impressed. She's going to love it," Frost admitted as he smiled and congratulated Ace and for managing to keep Alex in the dark. The team was well aware of Alex's ability to sniff out things.

"When is she supposed to be here?" Irish asked.

Ace looked at his watch. "In about thirty to forty-five minutes. She called a little while ago and said she was waiting for a phone call and then she'd be on her way. She thinks we're just having dinner."

5

Dino slapped him on the back. "Congratulations, man. It's about damn time."

Stitch walked over. "I can't believe it. I still remember the day you and Alex met. The surprised look on both of your faces when you guys realized you were working on the same mission was priceless."

Ace laughed. "Yeah. That had certainly caught me by surprise." When he was told their Intel Analyst's name was Alex, he had thought it was a guy."

Ace spotted Derek standing over by the bar. He excused himself and walked over. Derek shook his hand.

"I have to admit, Ace, you've outdone yourself. This is amazing. Alex isn't going to know what to think."

"I hope so. I think I've put Campbell and Arianna through the grinder with putting tonight together."

Derek laughed. "I'm sure they loved helping you put this together. I can't believe that Dino or Diego never caught on."

"The women of this team have their own sneaky skills.

"That they do."

"You know, I have to admit, hiding this from Alex has been killing me. I could tell she knew something was up, but she just couldn't quite put her finger on it."

"Ace, you know as well as I do that it's almost impossible to keep anything from that woman."

"She's amazing. I wish we could've met sooner than we did."

"She's one of a kind. I can tell you that." Derek looked away for a moment, and Ace could sense something that Derek wasn't saying.

"I know that look, Commander. What's on your mind?"

Derek offered him a wry smirk. "I'm glad this is happening."

Ace cocked his head sideways, not understanding. "What do you mean?"

"The wedding." Derek sighed. "I ran into Alex earlier today at the cemetery. I felt a bit bad for eavesdropping while she was talking to her dad."

6

Ace started to feel concerned. "What was she talking about?"

"Pretty much everything. But what bothered me was when she said she felt that you and she weren't aligned."

"What?"

"She went on about you both living hectic lives and how she's been under a lot of stress with the Foundation and the possible expansion out west."

Ace ran his hand through his hair. It was something he had been doing a lot lately.

"I get the stress part, but I really thought that having Charlie at the office would help ease some of it."

"I think it has. But you know how anxious she's been since that group from Coronado called. That's a lot. But I'm damn proud of her."

"I am too. She's doing amazing things, that's for sure."

Derek slapped him on the back and smiled. "Listen, don't sweat it. I think after tonight, you'll see a huge positive shift in her."

"I hope so."

# CHAPTER THREE

"Alex had just started to pack up her things for the night when her office phone rang." She sighed. She wanted to get out of there and go meet Ace for dinner. The call earlier that she had been expecting took a little longer than she had anticipated. But she couldn't complain, considering the organization had pledged a twelve thousand dollar donation. She reached across the desk and answered.

She looked at the phone number on the screen, and her gut did a little flip flop when she saw it was a San Diego area code.

"This is Alex."

"Alex. This Admiral Dietrich from Coronado."

She smiled. "Hello, Admiral. How are you?"

"Oh, you know. Doing just fine for a soon to be retired Admiral."

"Well, from what I've heard, you deserve that retirement."

He barked out a laugh. "Yeah, my wife says the same thing, but we'll see what she thinks in about six months."

Alex chuckled. "Oh, I'm sure she'll be tickled pink to have you at home."

"We'll have to see about that." He cleared his throat. "Anyway, I'm sorry to call you so late in the evening, but a few of the other board members and I met earlier to talk about your Foundation and what all your organization could bring to the community here in Coronado and the surrounding area."

Alex held her breath. This was it. They had made a decision—or so she thought.

"Okay."

"The group and I would like to meet with you in person to discuss a proposal."

She pulled up her calendar. "Okay. When are you thinking?"

"The day after tomorrow."

Her eyes bugged out of her head. *Holy shit!*

8

"I know it's extremely short notice, but two of our board members are leaving to head out of the country on Friday, and we would like to make a final decision before they go. And the only way we can do that is if we can all meet face-to-face."

She scanned her calendar, and the appointments and meetings she had booked were all reschedulable.

"Umm...I think I can make it work. Can you give me just a minute and let me check?

"Absolutely."

She pulled up the airline's website and searched for flights leaving the next day. She found two in the early afternoon that had plenty of seats left.

"Okay. I can make it work."

"Outstanding. Let me reach out to the board and get a time and location, and I'll email you all the details."

"Sounds like a plan."

"Alright. Then I guess I'll see you the day after tomorrow. And, Alex?"

"Yes, sir?"

"Just a heads up—the entire board is excited about this."

She grinned even though he couldn't see her. "That's wonderful to hear, sir. I'm thrilled as well."

"Talk to you later."

"Thank you for calling."

"Bye now."

"Bye."

As soon as Alex hung the phone on the receiver, she did a fist pump into the air. If the board wanted to meet in person to discuss the proposal, that meant the expansion was pretty much in the bag.

She sat down in her chair and rubbed her temples, trying to massage some of the tension out.

When she first launched her idea for the Foundation, her expectation was to assist the local military and veterans within the local area. She had never expected the tremendous outpouring of support she had received from all over the country. What they were doing was truly making a difference in someone's life, and she couldn't be any prouder of her staff and volunteers who have helped to promote and grow the Foundation to a national level.

She had a lot to think about. While the news of the Coronado location was great, the issue now was finding the right person to lead it. It had to be someone who shared and believed in the same values she had—someone who would take it and fly with it.

She heard the knock on her door, and when she looked towards the doorway, she smiled. Her answer stood right in front of her—Charlotte Taylor, or Charlie as she liked to be called.

Charlie was a godsend to the Foundation. When Alex sought someone to manage the day-to-day business, Charlie appeared out of nowhere and ran with it.

Charlie knew firsthand what our military service members, veterans, and their families face in a time of need. Her life had been turned upside down a few years ago when her dad, a Lt. Colonel in the Army, had perished in a helicopter crash in the mountains of Afghanistan. But her tragedies didn't end there. Her brother, a Marine with the 11th Marine Expeditionary Unit out of California, suffered from severe depression after he returned home from serving two back-to-back deployments in the Middle East. During the last deployment, his unit had been ambushed, resulting in the tragic deaths of over half of his fellow soldiers—many of whom were good friends. Charlie tried to help him as much as she could, but it wasn't enough. Sadly, her brother took his own life. From that day on, Charlie vowed that she would do whatever it took not to let another soldier feel as if they had nothing to live for.

"Hey, Charlie."

"Hi. I just wanted to let you know that I was heading out. I think you're the only one left."

Alex thought about her call with Admiral Dietrich. Even though it wasn't official yet, it couldn't hurt to plant the seed.

"Hey, before you go, do you have a quick minute? There's something I want to run by you."

10

"Sure." She stepped into the office and took a seat in the chair in front of the desk. "Is everything okay?"

Alex smiled. "Yes. In fact, I just received some positive news from Coronado. Fingers crossed that the project gets the green light in a few days."

Charlie's eyes lit up, and that was all that Alex needed to see. "Alex, that's fantastic. You've put so much blood and sweat into making this happen."

"Well, it's not quite official yet, but the board of the organization backing it wants to meet with me the day after tomorrow."

Alex explained everything, and Charlies appeared enthusiastic, which was another positive sign.

"However, if the board approves it on Friday, they are going to want to hit the ground running."

Charlie furrowed her brows. "What's wrong with that?"

"Nothing's wrong with it. It's just I can't be in two places at once."

"Oh."

"Charlie, you've done a tremendous job in the little time you've been here. How would you like to take on a more prominent role with the Foundation?"

"What did you have in mind?"

"A Director position. Specifically, the Director of the Coronado site."

"What? Are you sure you want me to run it?"

"I'm sure as I'll ever be," Alex said with a smile.

Charlie sat back in the chair, and Alex watched her closely. This would be a fantastic opportunity for Charlie, mainly since she talked about moving back to California.

Charlie focused on work to keep her mind busy. And if she could save one life in her outreach, then that was all that mattered.

"Charlie, I know it's a big decision to make, but believe me, if I didn't think you could handle it, I wouldn't have offered it to you. You are wonderful at what you do. Because of your own experiences, you can relate to those who are seeking help. If you want to sleep on it and—"

11

Charlie sat up straight. "I'll take it."

Alex smiled. "Really?"

"Really. You know I've been talking with my Aunt and Uncle in San Diego and contemplating making a move back out there. With this opportunity, I can and still do what I love doing—helping people."

"Yes, you can."

"I don't know what to say. I mean, thank you, of course."

"No thanks needed. You earned it, and I know you'll do great. How about we talk more next week after I get back."

"Sounds wonderful." Charlie stood up. "Remember, I'm out of the office tomorrow and Friday, so I'll see you on Monday."

"Got it. Enjoy your time off."

Alex couldn't stop smiling as she watched Charlie practically skip out of the office. This was going to be great.

Alex looked at the time. Damn, she was going to be a few minutes late. She couldn't wait to tell him the good news, minus the part she had to travel out to California. She shut her laptop down and stuffed it into her bag, grabbed her purse and keys, then headed for the door. Tonight she was going to celebrate.

# CHAPTER FOUR

Alex pulled into the parking lot at Bayside. Her mind was running rampant. She needed to chill. But it was hard. She was a planner and liked things in an orderly fashion. The spontaneous phone call from Coronado had put a wrench in her style.

She grabbed her purse and got out of the car. As she walked toward the entrance, she noticed many familiar vehicles in the parking lot, and she wondered if her and Ace's dinner turned into a team dinner.

She pulled open the door and looked around but didn't see anyone, not even Ace. She spotted Paul by the bar, and he came around hugged her.

"Ace is in the back room. He was taking a phone call. You can go ahead back there."

She smiled. "Thanks."

As she made her way down the hall and made a left into the room, she about had a heart attack when everyone shouted.

"Surprise!"

The first and only time until now that anyone surprised her with a party had been in Afghanistan when the team surprised her on her birthday. She had no clue what was going on, but all of her and Ace's friends, her uncles, Ace's family, hell, everyone close to them were there. As she scanned the room, something seemed very familiar—the look and feel of the room. Then it clicked. It was almost identical to the picture she had found to replicate for her and Ace's wedding rehearsal dinner, but with a few added touches. There were pictures of her and Ace placed all around the room. She sought Ace out. As soon as she laid eyes on him, she about burst into tears.

He strode towards her and leaned down, and kissed her. When he released her lips, she opened her eyes stared up at him. She opened her mouth to say something, but no words would come out. She swallowed hard. *Get it together.*

"Ace, what's going on? What is this?"

13

He wrapped his arms around her waist and gazed into her eyes. His blue eyes were like crystals as they sparkled with excitement.

"Since I met you, all I've ever wanted is for you to be my wife, my equal, my other half. I know how hard it's been for you to stand on the sidelines as our friends and even family all got their happily ever after. But now it's your turn."

"Ace, what are you saying."

He grinned. "Say that on Saturday you'll meet me at that chapel where you originally wanted to get married and walk down the aisle and officially become Mrs. Marcus Chambers."

Tears pooled in her eyes. This was the sweetest thing he had ever done, and that said a lot because he had already done some amazing things.

She took a deep breath as her tears spilled over and ran down her cheeks.

"It's all I've ever wanted since meeting you. I love you so much." She pulled him close. "I want nothing more than to become Mrs. Marcus Chambers." She hugged him again and buried her face in his neck.

When she eased back, she looked around the room again and seeing all the smiles on everyone's faces warmed her heart. She then took Ace's hand.

"Are we really getting married this weekend?" she asked, then pinched herself to make sure she wasn't dreaming, and Ace laughed.

"By two o'clock Saturday afternoon, you and I will officially be married."

She wiped her eyes again because the tears didn't want to stop, and that was okay because they were happy tears.

"You don't know how happy I am right now." She felt as if she was going to explode with all the excitement that was building in her.

"How did you have time to do all this? Did everyone know about it?"

He smiled. "Derek knew since I started planning it. The only other two who knew were Arianna and Campbell. But they found out about two weeks ago, and it was only to help with tonight. Nobody else knew. They were all just as surprised when they got here."

"I can't believe this." Her cheeks were already starting to hurt from smiling.

Derek walked over and handed her a Malibu and Pineapple. "I thought you might need this," he teased before he gave her a big hug, which of course, made her start crying again. When he pulled back, he looked down into her eyes and smiled. "See, I told you earlier that everything would work out."

She grinned. "Yes, you did."

"You deserve this and so much more. I can't tell you how happy I am for you and Ace."

"Thank you."

He hugged her again, and then everyone started approaching them and offering their congratulations.

Before long, everyone was eating, drinking, sharing stories of Ace and Alex, and enjoying the evening. Alex couldn't get enough of baby Aiden, Frost, and Autumn's newborn. He was the spitting image of Frost except for his hair. He had more of Autumn's auburn color. As she held him in her arms, she sought out Kensi and Kelsey, Potter and Tenley's twins. When she spotted Arianna and Mia holding them, she grinned. It was just a matter of time before everyone was having babies.

She suddenly felt an odd sensation in her belly. She wondered how long before she and Ace would start trying. They both had decided that they would wait until they got married. If it were up to her, they would start making that baby Saturday night. Ace had told her that their honeymoon was a surprise.

She then remembered that with all of the excitement, she hadn't told anyone about her good news. After she kissed baby Aiden on the cheek, she handed him back over to Frost. God, just watching those big muscular men hold those babies were enough to send her ovaries into overdrive.

Alex spotted Ace talking to his mom and Colonel Johnson. She was happy that Ace's mom had found a special someone, and Colonel Johnson was a great guy. Alex had the opportunity to work alongside him in Afghanistan.

As she approached the group, Ace smiled.

"Hey, sweetheart. We were just talking about you."

15

She tilted her head. "You were?"

"Ace was just updating Mike and me on the expansion for the Foundation."

Alex smiled. "Well, actually, that was what I was coming here for." She looked at Ace. "With all the excitement around here, I didn't get a chance to tell you that I received a phone call from Admiral Dietrich."

Ace stood up. "And…"

She couldn't hide her excitement. "I think it's a go."

"Seriously?!"

She nodded her head. "Seriously. The only catch is that I have to fly to Coronado to meet with the board face-to-face."

Ace's smile faded. "When?"

She bit her lip, knowing this would make him worry now that she knew what he planned. "Tomorrow."

Ace's eyes widened. "Tomorrow? When will you be back?"

"As long as everything stays on schedule, I fly out tomorrow, meet with the board on Thursday, and then fly home on Friday." She took Ace's hands and pulled him closer to her. "Then Saturday, I get to marry my best friend."

He hugged her. "That's kind of cutting it close, isn't it?" He asked, and she agreed. It was cutting it very close. With the way airlines operated and unknown weather delays, there was always a slight possibility that she may not make it back in time. But the odds were low.

Before she could respond, Derek and Tink joined them. Ace asked if she had told them the good news, and she explained that she had wanted to tell him first. Both Derek and Tink were over the moon that the expansion had moved into the proposal stage.

"Alex, I'm heading out there tomorrow as well," Tink told her.

"You are?"

"Yeah. I'm meeting a couple of other guys out there. There's a Security Industry tradeshow on Thursday in San Diego. I'm taking the jet, so if you want to ride with me, I've got more than enough room."

She smiled. "That would be great. What time are you leaving?"

He shrugged his broad shoulders. "When I tell the pilot when I want to leave."

She laughed. "Let me rephrase the question. What time were you thinking of leaving?"

He grinned. "Around noonish. Would that work for you?"

"Absolutely."

"The trade show lasts pretty late. Are you good if we left to come home early on Friday, say depart around o five hundred?"

Alex did the math in her head. If they left at five o'clock in the morning, pacific time, and the flight is roughly five hours—with the time change, they should arrive in Virginia Beach sometime between one and two o'clock. That would give her plenty of time to get ready for the following day, especially since all she needed to do was show up.

"I think it sounds like the perfect plan."

She walked over and hugged Tink. "Thank you."

He winked. "I do anything to make sure our princess is back in time to marry her prince."

Alex, and Ace both, groaned and rolled their eyes. Tink laughed while Derek stood there shaking his head.

"That was cheezy. You know that, right?" Derek said to Tink, but Tink didn't care. He just shrugged his shoulders.

It was late when Alex noticed that Ace wasn't anywhere in sight. Most of the guests had already gone home, but a few of the guys had stayed and were sitting at one of the tables with Bear and a few guys from his team. She caught Potter's eye, and as if knowing who she was seeking out, he nodded toward the beach.

Once she made it outside and down the pathway to the beach, she slipped off her shoes and left them by the stairs before she made her way toward the water where Ace stood.

It was a clear night with a light breeze blowing in off the ocean. As she approached, he turned and flashed her a smile. He held his hand out for her

17

to take. She slipped her hand in his and snuggled into his side. They stood like that for minutes watching as the moon rose over the vast ocean.

She heard him take a deep breath.

"Everything okay?" She asked.

He squeezed her a little tighter.

"I just realized something," he told her, and she looked up at him as he glanced down at her.

"What's that?"

"When you leave tomorrow, that will be the first time that you've left me."

She wrinkled her forehead. "What do you mean? I've gone on business trips before."

"Yeah, but you took those when I was either deployed or at a training."

She thought about that for a minute, and he was right.

"I never realized that either."

He took another deep breath and released it. "God, is this how you feel when I leave?"

"I don't know. How do you feel right now?"

He shrugged his shoulders. "A guess a sense of loneliness knowing you won't be home when I get off from work, or you won't be there next to me in bed when I wake up. And I always worry about you, so there's that too."

She smiled. "I guess it's sort of the same. But it's not just when you're being deployed. It's every single day you walk out of the house because I know in the back of my mind that you could get called out at a moment's notice. Sometimes even without enough time for me to say goodbye."

He ran his knuckles down her cheek. "I'm sorry."

"Don't be sorry. I knew what I was signing up for when I fell in love with you."

"Fuck…"

He pulled her in front of him and cupped her face as he looked into her emerald green eyes.

"I cannot wait until Saturday, and you become my wife—my partner."

18

"Ace, I've always wanted to be your wife." She felt the tears building in her eyes. "Why in the hell did we wait so long?" she asked.

"Because I wanted to give you the wedding of your dreams."

"None of that mattered." She tapped his chest, right over his heart. "You already gave me this. That was all I needed."

"I love you," he said and kissed her.

She closed her eyes, feeling the love he put forth into the kiss.

When he pulled back just a smidge, she gave him a cheeky smile. "Do you love me enough to tell me where we're going for our honeymoon?"

He barked a loud laugh then kissed her again. This time it was a quick touch of his lips.

"Nice try."

She then got serious. "I never thanked you yet for putting all of this together. I'm truly touched by it."

He pulled her close. "You don't have to thank me. I'd do anything for you."

She looked up at him. "Just as I'd do for you."

He smiled. "How about a walk on the beach before we head home. I have plenty of ideas in mind on what you can do for me there," he said as he playfully raised his eyebrows.

She shook her head. "You're crazy."

"Crazy for you, sweetheart."

As they started to walk, she remembered something she wanted to ask him about.

"What was with the big stuffed pink rabbit that Sienna had with her tonight?"

Ace chuckled and shook his head. I was sworn to secrecy," he said, but still laughing, and Alex knew whatever the story was behind the pink rabbit had to be good.

Alex stopped him from walking and pressed her body against his. She got up on her tiptoes and began kissing his chin, then his cheek before reaching his ear. She gently sucked on his earlobe.

"Are you sure that there is nothing I can do for you to let me in on the secret? You know I'm good at keeping secrets," she whispered.

She placed her hand on his hip and started to run it towards his cock when he grabbed her wrist. When she looked up and met his eyes, she thought she would need a firehose to douse the fire and intensity burning through them.

"You are playing with fire," he said. His voice was low and raspy, which drove her crazy, and was so hot that it melted her insides. "If you don't want anyone out on this beach to hear your cries of pleasure, I suggest that you and I turn around right now and head home because I am seconds from being inside you."

She squeezed her thighs together as she panted heavily. She felt so aroused. When she looked up at him and didn't say anything, he just gave her that sexy look with one eyebrow raised.

"I don't think I can walk," she finally admitted, and he chuckled before picking her up and throwing her over his shoulder. They only stopped for her to grab her purse.

# CHAPTER FIVE

Ace was beside himself. The way Alex looked at him and whispered sexual innuendos into his ear made his cock throb. It had been an uncomfortable ride home for sure.

He pulled his truck into the drive and sprinted into the house. Zuma, of course, was waiting at the front door. The dog loved attention because Alex spoiled him. Hurriedly Ace let Zuma outside to do his business while he grabbed a beer from the refrigerator.

As he stood on the back porch in the dark while he waited for the damn dog to sniff every fucking bush until he found the perfect one to pee on, he didn't think it would hurt to start undressing. He pulled his shirt over his head. Next, he toed off his shoes, then popped the button on his jeans. He had them lowered to just around his knees when he heard someone clear their throat.

He closed his eyes and thanked the lord he hadn't taken his underwear down with the jeans. He looked over his shoulder and saw Tenley standing out on her back porch with a shit-eating grin on her face. He knew he was screwed.

"I didn't think the full moon was supposed to be until tomorrow night," she teased, trying to hold back her laughter.

He groaned, then stood up straight and quickly pulled his jeans back up. Christ, she was going to hold this over his head for a long time.

He called for Zuma, and the pup came. Before ducking back inside the house, he shouted over the fence. "Night, Tenley." As he closed the door, he could still hear her laughing.

Shaking his head, he got Zuma settled in the game room. On his way through the house, he got his phone and checked the tracking app to see where Alex was. They had each other's phones programmed in the app. His phone, of course, was deactivated when he would deploy.

He saw that Alex was just leaving Bayside. He rolled his eyes and damned Arianna for stopping her when they were trying to leave.

21

He headed up the stairs to their bedroom. Knowing he had a good ten minutes, he jumped in a quick shower. After he was showered, he wrapped a towel around his waist. There was no use putting clothes on when they were going to just come right back off in a matter of minutes.

He turned the lights down low and turned down the bed. He found the TV remote and turned on one of the music channels. He thought about something wild like some rock-n-roll since he was feeling a little wild. But then he reconsidered. He wanted tonight to be special and memorable, especially for Alex. So, he found a channel that played some light jazz. He looked around and smiled. The ambiance in the room was perfect.

He heard the front door open and close. He waited on pins and needles, praying that she wouldn't go looking for the dog. When he heard her purse fall and hit the tile floor and the sound of her kicking off her shoes, he realized she must feeling what he was.

Moments later, she sauntered into the bedroom. He absorbed the sight of her. Her hair was all windblown from their walk on the beach, and her blouse was half unbuttoned, revealing an abundance of her cleavage. Jesus, she looked gorgeous and so tempting. He found himself licking his lips.

She looked him over and grinned before she started to walk toward him.

He didn't say anything as he took her hands and held them behind her back with one of his hands. He watched as her chest rose and fell with each breath she took. He used his other hand to hold her head in place as he covered her mouth and kissed her deeply.

The feel of her body so close to his fueled his need to possess her body. As he continued to kiss her, she moaned against his mouth. When he finally released her lips, he couldn't hold back his smile. She looked well-loved. Her lips were swollen and red, and her cheeks flushed.

She started to unbutton her shirt, but he stopped her. "Let me."

She placed her hands to her sides and stared at him as he slowly undid her blouse. Every button he released revealed a glimpse of her tanned belly.

Suddenly, visions of her with a rounded belly came to his mind. She would look gorgeous carrying their child.

"Ace?" she questioned, and he looked into her eyes.

22

He placed one of his hands on her belly. "I can't wait for you to be pregnant with our baby."

He saw her eyes start to glisten.

"I can't wait either," she said, placing her hand over his. "I love you," she told him and kissed his bare chest right over his heart.

The sound of her soft, silky voice had him trying to maintain his composure.

Alex closed her eyes as she pressed her cheek against Ace's bare chest. She couldn't believe how happy she was. If anyone would've asked her two years ago as she stepped on that airplane bound for Afghanistan, if she would find her future husband, she would've thought that it was the funniest joke. As much as she would love to put that trip out of her mind, she couldn't. How could she when it was there that she had met the man of her dreams? The man who in three days would become her husband.

Ace pushed her blouse off her shoulder then kissed her bare skin. His touch sent tingles all through her body. She was lost in sensation as he ran his hands down her bare back to waist.

As she tilted her chin up toward him, he kissed her again. For some reason, she was feeling unusually emotional. Her eyes kept tearing up, and he was so sweet and would wipe them away.

She began to relax more into his touch as he moved his hands to the front of her dress pants and undid the button. His movements were methodical. As he lowered her pants, he kissed along her belly then down lower. She sucked in a deep breath as she felt his warm breath over her mound. She ran her fingers through his thick hair.

Once he had her pants off, he reached around to her back and unclipped her bra. When the lacy material fell to the ground, and she was left standing there in just her thong panties, he eyed her over with a hunger in his eyes.

"Stunning," he rasped out.

Even after two years of being intimate with him, he still managed to make her blush.

He took her into his arms and lifted her. He walked them over to the bed, and he gently laid her down before he covered her with his body.

When she felt his cock tap against her pussy she thought she would explode right then. As he placed kisses all over her body, the sensations inside were unbearable. She needed him so badly.

As if reading her mind, he sat up and removed her panties. He stared at her. His gaze was carnal and intense.

"The day we locked gazes in that chow hall in the desert, I knew you were meant to be mine," he told her.

"I will always be yours, Ace."

"Damn right you will."

He hovered over her and took her lips in another mind-blowing, orgasmic kiss that left her feeling limp. As he released her lips, he settled his body between her thighs. Moments later, she felt his cock slowly pushing inside her. She was already panting. It felt so good.

As he thrust his hips slowly, she ran her hands up his chest and over his broad, muscular shoulders. She craved everything about him. She felt that familiar butterfly sensation in her belly and knew she was close. Three more strokes, and he bumped that special button inside her that sent her reeling into another universe—it was almost magical.

Ace followed moments later and released himself inside her. He collapsed on top of her but held most of his weight off of her.

He kissed her tenderly, and she cupped his face.

"How did I get so lucky?" She asked him.

He smiled and turned his head and kissed the palm of her hand. "I think the question is, how did I get so lucky. You are everything I had ever hoped for in finding a woman. You are one amazing woman, Alexandra Hardesty."

Ace rolled to his side and brought her with him, and she curled into his side. Just as she was about to doze off, she remembered there was something she was supposed to ask him.

"Ace?"

"Yeah?"

"Tenley asked me to remind you to let her know when the next full moon was."

# CHAPTER SIX

The following evening, Alex and Tink decided to grab a bite to eat at their hotel. They were going to stay near the convention center but then decided to head over to Hotel del Coronado. Alex didn't object because she loved Hotel del Coronado. Being near the Naval Amphibious base there in Coronado made her feel a little closer to Ace even though they were two thousand seven hundred twenty-four miles apart. Ace had made sure to tell her the exact mileage before she left.

Just as they sat down at their table, Tink raised his hand and waved to someone. When Alex turned to look, she saw a large, brown-haired guy walking towards them. Just from his posture and gait, she knew he had to have been former military.

Tink glanced at her. I forgot to mention that I invited a friend of mine to have dinner with us. He's in town for the tradeshow as well.

Alex smiled. "It's fine. You know I love meeting your friends."

Tink smirked. "Yeah. More like interrogate."

Alex chuckled. "You do realize that a lot of those interrogations saved my ass when I worked in the field."

Tink's smirked disappeared. "I don't want to think about you working in the field."

She reached across the table and patted his hand. "Now, you know those days are behind me."

"Thank God," she heard him mumble under his breath just as their dinner guest arrived at the table.

Tink stood up, and the two guys hugged in what Alex would call a man hug. Tink then looked at Alex.

"Alex, I'd like for you to meet Mac Ramsey. Mac, this is Alex, Jake's little girl."

The guy Mac stepped forward and shook her hand. "I remember you when you were just a little bundle of joy in your daddy's arms. I had the pleasure of knowing your dad and serving with him on a couple of tours."

26

She smiled, and Tink spoke as he slapped Mac on the shoulder. "Yeah, Mac here was stationed on the West Coast. He and I went through BUD/S together. He retired a couple of years ago and just recently moved to Florida and opened his own security business.

She shook his hand. "It's nice to meet you as well."

Mac and Tink both took their seats, and then the waitress took their drink orders.

"So, Mac, where in Florida are you headquartered?" Alex asked.

The waitress brought over their drinks, and Mac took a sip of his before he answered. "St. Augustine."

Alex smiled. "Nice. Although, I don't think I get any work done. St. Augustine is beautiful and filled with so much history. What made you pick there?"

Mac grinned. "For the same reasons you just stated. And I grew up there."

"Do you still have family there?"

"No. I was an only child, and my parents died a few years ago," he explained.

"I'm sorry to hear that," she offered.

"Me too," he replied rather terse but not directed at her. She sensed there was more to that story, and she wasn't going to press the issue.

"Well, maybe Ace and I'll visit one day when we get a break."

He smiled. "Absolutely." He looked at Tink then back to her. "You both have an open invitation. I've got plenty of room and would love to host you guys." He smirked. "Maybe I'll give Ace a tour of our headquarters."

Alex laughed. "If you were thinking of recruiting him, you'll probably be waiting a few years. Ace is committed to his team, and I don't see him leaving the teams any time soon. At least not if he can help it."

Mac grinned. "Hey, a guy's gotta try."

"Yes, they do."

As the evening went off, Alex was enjoying herself. She really liked Mac. He was a unique character. Even though he conversed, at times, he appeared to be reserved.

"You've got to be kidding me," Tink uttered from across the table as he looked at something over Alex's shoulder. Before she could ask what was wrong, he excused himself.

She turned and tried to follow him with her eyes, but he disappeared over by the bar. She turned around and looked at Mac.

"That was weird," she said, and Mac nodded.

While she and Mac waited for Tink to return, they talked more about her Foundation.

"What you're doing is vital to our men and women and is commendable," he told her.

"Thank you. It's something close to me."

"You're dad would be so proud of you. He was an honorable man."

She didn't know how to respond because her emotions were starting to choke her up, so she offered him a smile. He seemed to understand.

He then looked around.

"Do you think maybe we should go look for him?"

Alex scanned the restaurant, and she didn't see him either. They had already paid the bill.

"Sure, why not."

As they made their way out of the restaurant, they spotted Tink in the lobby. He was standing with a woman, and judging from his body language; he didn't seem pleased with her. His body was tense, and he stood with his arms crossed in front of his chest.

She debated on whether or not she should go over. Just as she decided that she'd give them some space, Tink and the woman turned in her direction. As soon as Alex met the woman's gaze, Alex felt as if her world had just been rocked. There was no way in hell that her mother was standing across the room from her—the same mother who walked out on her husband and a six-month-old baby.

*What the ever-loving fuck was happening?*

"Tink?" Alex questioned. Alex had even realized that she had tears in her eyes. But they weren't happy tears.

Before Tink could say anything, the woman brushed past Tink.

"Alexandra, is that really you?" The woman said.

Tink came over and stood next to Alex, which she was thankful for because she had no idea what even to say. This had come out of the left field. What were the flipping odds that she would run into her mother?

Tink draped his arm over her shoulders.

"Alex. This is Nora."

The woman started to reach out but caught herself, and it was a good thing because Alex wasn't sure how she wanted this to play out. Growing up, she had always wondered if she'd ever had the opportunity to meet her mom. But now that the time had arrived, she wasn't sure how she felt about it—confused was the front runner, but anger came in a close second.

She closed her eyes for a moment to gather herself. Her dad and uncles raised her not to be a bitter person. They taught her that even though forgiveness won't erase the past, it will help you heal in most situations.

Alex looked up at Tink and gave him a slight nod, letting him know that she got this. She stepped forward and held her hand out.

"It's nice to meet you, Nora."

When the woman placed her hand in Alex's, Alex had expected to feel something, but there was nothing. It was as if she was meeting a stranger.

"Oh, my." The woman said with tears in her eyes. "You look so much like him." Alex knew she was referring to her dad. "I was sorry to hear about his passing."

That last statement stung. Alex wondered when Nora knew about her ex-husband's death. Had it been when the State of Virginia was threatening to put her in a foster home?

"It was a difficult time. My dad was my world—my rock. Losing him hurt a great deal." Alex peered up at Tink and softly smiled. "But aside from losing my dad, I wouldn't have traded my childhood for anything. I was raised by some of the greatest men I'll ever know in my lifetime. Those men are my family.

"Alex, I'm so sorry."

Alex held her hand up to stop her.

"Nora, I'm not looking for apologies. I'm sure you had your reasons for your actions. It happened, and everyone involved has moved on."

Nora's eyes started to widen as she looked at something past Alex. When Alex turned, she spotted two girls who looked to be in their late teens or early twenties. They were walking with a man—a man wearing a Navy Summer White uniform. She noticed the gold wings device he wore over his service ribbons.

"That's my family."

Alex thought her jaw was going to hit the floor. This was a woman who left a man in the Navy because she said she couldn't handle the stress of his deployments. But then married another man in the Navy who was an aviator and probably did just as many deployments?

Alex turned back toward Nora. She didn't know what to say.

"Alex. They don't know about you. Well, my husband does, but Kendra and Kara don't. At least not yet. I had hoped that one day the girls could meet their half-sister."

Alex could see the remorse in Nora's eyes. Before the trio made it to them, Alex said, "If it's forgiveness you are seeking, then you are forgiven, but I don't think I can be a part of your life."

Alex looked at Tink. "I need some air." As Alex walked toward the sliding doors that led out to the beach, she couldn't bring herself to take one last look at the woman who had given her life, knowing it would most likely be the last time she ever saw her again.

# CHAPTER SEVEN

Ace walked out onto the deck and took a seat at the patio table. The guys had tried to get him to go up to Bayside for a drink, but he opted to stay home. He picked up the bottle of beer and took a swig. The bitter taste of the IPA brew matched his current mood.

He leaned back in the cushioned chair and looked up at the larger and brighter supermoon in the sky. He smiled to himself, wondering if Alex could see it. She loved sitting out on the patio to star and moon gaze.

His heart felt empty without her there at home. He heard Zuma's nails clicking on the composite decking as he walked over. He laid his head on Ace's lap. Ace grinned as he scratched the chocolate lab behind his ears.

"I know, buddy. I miss her too." As if Zuma understood what he said, he released a small whimper.

Before Ace even heard the gate between their yard and Potter and Tenley's yard open, Zuma emitted a low growl. But when Potter appeared from behind the gate, Zuma trotted over to greet him with a wagging tail.

After giving Zuma, some loving Potter climbed the steps to the deck and took the seat across from Ace.

"I figured you would be out here." Potter followed Ace's line of sight and looked up at the sky. "That is one gorgeous moon."

Ace nodded his head. "That it is."

Ace looked at Potter. Potter was his brother from another mother. He was someone that he shared everything with.

"Did you hear about Bear's sister?" Potter asked.

Ace tilted his head sideways. "No. What's going on?"

"Apparently, her helicopter went down somewhere over Mexico. The details area real sketchy right now."

Ace sat up straight. "What? Clover?"

Potter nodded.

"I thought she was a mechanic?" Ace asked.

31

"Me too. As I said, there's not much information being provided. Last I heard, they've listed Clover and who I'm assuming the pilot as MIA."

"Shit. I bet Bear's dad isn't taking the lack of information well."

"Irish was the one who spoke with Bear. He said none of the family was taking the news well."

"Damn. I hope she's alright."

Potter set his bottle down. "So, how are you holding up here all by yourself?"

Ace leaned his head back and glanced back up toward the sky. "Is this how the women feel every time we get called out?"

Potter snickered. "Most likely. But I think our women are a lot stronger than we give them credit for. You, me, and the rest of the guys are accustomed to being the ones leaving. Hell, I still have a hard time if Tenley has to work a double at the hospital."

Ace smirked. "It sucks."

"That it does, my friend."

Just then, Ace's phone rang. When he saw Derek's name, his gut clenched.

"Hey, Commander."

"Hey. Sorry to bother you, but two things." Hearing Derek sigh was never a good sign.

"What's going on?"

"First, did you hear about Bear's sister?"

"Yeah. Potter's here and he just told me. That's terrible."

"It is. I'm trying to get some information, but it hasn't been easy. The government is being tight-lipped."

"Hmmm…that is strange."

"If and when I hear anything, I'll let you know."

"Okay."

"The second this is, have you heard from Alex yet?"

"I heard from her when she called earlier after they arrived."

"Shit. So you haven't heard what went down at dinner?"

Ace sat up, and it caught Potter's eye too. "No. What happened? Is she okay?"

"Physically, she's fine, but she ran into her mother at the hotel restaurant."

*Oh, fuck!*

"How?" Ace asked.

"Apparently, she lives out there. She remarried and has two daughters."

Ace knew Alex was probably devastated.

"Have you spoken with her?" Ace asked.

"No. Tink called me. He said that Alex went for a walk to get some air."

"Shit."

"Exactly. Anyway, I thought you should know so when she calls."

He wasn't waiting around for her to call. As soon as he hung up with Derek, he was calling her.

"Alright. I'll let you know after I talk with her."

"Thanks."

Ace disconnected the call and threw the phone onto the table. Potter raised his eyebrows in question.

"Alex ran into her mother tonight at the hotel."

"You've got to be kidding me?" Potter stated.

"Derek said Tink called him."

"Is she okay?"

"Don't know. Tink said she went for a walk."

Potter stood up. "Well, go ahead and give her a call. I have to get back to the house as well. I told Tenley I'd bathe the babies tonight."

"Sounds like fun," Ace teased.

As Potter started down the stairs, he turned back. "I almost forgot, and I have no idea what she means, but she said that you would know. But Tenley told me to tell you that the full moon tonight is better than the last one she saw."

Ace had to hide his smile. "Tell her I said thanks."

Potter just shook his head. "Talk to you later, man."

"See ya."

33

Ace was concerned for Alex. He picked up the phone and dialed her number.

Alex sat on the beach with her toes buried in the diamond white sand as she looked out on the horizon. The flaming orange sun slowly dipped into the water as the super moon rose into the sky. It was a gorgeous night with clear skies and a perfect seventy-five degrees.

She heard some shouting and looked to the left and smiled as several groups of men in their uniforms walked down the beach carrying zodiacs above their heads—SEALs in training. It was a large group, but she knew that half of them would be left standing and earning the famed trident pin by the end of their training.

She had so much respect for the men and women who even attempted the program.

The unexpected meeting with her mother had taken a toll on her mentally. She still couldn't believe that she had remarried another Naval Officer or the fact that she had two daughters. She lowered her head and closed her eyes.

The buzzing of her phone drew her out of the fog she was in. The name flashing across the screen made her heart skip a beat, and tears welled in her eyes. She'd do anything to have Ace with her right now. She swiped the screen connecting her to the man who owned her heart completely.

"Hi," she greeted him.

"Hey, sweetheart," his voice was low, and she knew that he already knew about the run-in with her mom.

"I guess Tink called you?" She asked.

"Derek did."

Alex wasn't surprised. She figured Tink would call Derek. She actually wondered how Derek took it. Even though Derek taught her about forgiveness, Derek was known to hold grudges when it came to certain people, and her mother was one of them.

"Are you okay?" Ace asked her.

34

"I'm actually doing better than I thought I'd be. Then again, that could be because of the two drinks I had before walking down the beach."

"You're at the beach?"

"Yeah."

"Isn't it getting dark there?"

"I'm good. Tink is watching my six." She smiled and turned her head back toward the hotel, and there was Tink, sitting on the pool deck. Any other person would think he was looking at the beautiful view in front of him, but she knew it was her he was watching. She would guarantee that if anyone came within twenty or so feet of her, he'd be at her side in a heartbeat.

"I wish I was there with you," he told her.

"I wish you were here too."

"How's Zuma?"

"He misses you too."

She smiled to herself.

"Ace?"

"Yeah, babe?"

"You know I love you, right?"

"Of course. Why would you even ask that?"

She sighed. "I think running into my mom made my mind go all wonky. I just want you to know that I'm not her. I would never leave you."

"Alex...sweetheart. That never even crossed my mind. I don't ever want to hear you compare yourself to that woman."

"Sorry."

"Don't be sorry. You are an amazing woman. I know I tell you that all the time. It would help if you started believing that.

She grinned. "You're so sweet. You know that?"

He chuckled. "Sweet, huh?"

"Yep, because I could just eat you up."

"Alex..." he said in warning. "You're not playing fair."

She laughed. "Alright. I'm sorry. That wasn't nice of me. I'll make it up to you when I get home."

"Now you're just torturing me."

"Well, then let me let you go. I'm going to head back up and see Tink."

"Alright. I love you," he told her.

"I love you, too, and I'll talk to you tomorrow."

"Goodnight, sweetheart."

"Night."

She disconnected, then stood up and brushed the sand off her pants before heading back up to the hotel. What she needed was a nice hot relaxing bath with lots of bubbles.

# CHAPTER EIGHT

The following day Alex sat in the conference room with Admiral Dietrich and the other six board members.

She was doing everything she could to hold in her excitement. The board had not only voted to greenlight the expansion, but they had surprised her when they told her that they were gifting her organization, not one but three vacant buildings to run the clinic and programs out of. The initial funding was already in place to begin renovating the complex, which would take about six months.

"Alex, I can't tell you enough how fortunate we are to have what you're offering to our community," Admiral Dietrich told her.

"If I could open a center in every community in this country, I would. Nobody, especially our men and woman who serve and protect, should have to worry about acquiring medical services."

"Well, we are excited."

"I am too. When I get back to my office, I pull together the information you need to hand over to the contractors. I'll also set up a call to introduce you to Charlie since she'll be overseeing this location."

Admiral Dietrich smiled. "I'm looking forward to it."

After saying goodbye to the other board members, Alex got into her rental and headed toward the hotel. As she was leaving the base, she saw a shopping plaza with a deli, and she pulled in. She hadn't eaten breakfast because she was so nervous, and with it being a little past three o'clock, she was starving.

She parked the car and walked into the store. It was reasonably large inside. She went up to the counter and ordered a turkey and cheese sandwich. While she waited, she walked to the back of the store to use the restroom.

As she was in one of the stalls, she heard the door open and two people were whispering. She couldn't make out what they were saying, but she thought it seemed a little weird.

37

After she flushed and fixed herself, she opened the stall door and met Kendra and Kara, her half-sisters.

At first, she wasn't sure what to say, and thankfully she didn't have to because Kendra spoke first.

"Alex. Please don't be upset with us."

Okay, Alex hadn't been expecting that, considering Nora had said that the girls didn't know about her.

Alex swallowed hard. "Why would I be upset with you girls? You've done nothing wrong."

"Mom told us about you," Kara chimed in.

"She did?" That surprised Alex.

Kendra nodded. "Yeah. We saw you with her, and after you left, mom was upset. She and dad pulled us and explained everything."

"Oh. I don't know what to say."

Then out of nowhere, they both hugged her. "Please tell us that you'll be our sister?"

Again, the tears started to build, and she couldn't speak over the emotion she was feeling. These girls were just innocent bystanders in a screwed-up situation. It wasn't fair to them. She then found herself hugging them back.

After a few moments, she pulled back and wiped the tears away, then looked at them and shook her head.

"First thing is first. How did you find me?"

The girls looked at each other. "Our dad told us about the Foundation you ran and mentioned that you were meeting with the board today, so we waited and followed you."

Alex chuckled. "Okay. Let me wash my hands and then how about if we go sit outside and talk?"

Both of the girls smiled.

As Alex began to wash her hands, the room started to shake. At first, she thought she had imagined it, but when she looked up, and one of the large light fixtures fell, she realized it wasn't her imagination. It was an earthquake. She jumped out of the way just in time as it came crashing down right where she had been standing. Kara and Kendra both screamed as the ceiling above them started to give way.

As concrete fell on them, Alex pulled both girls into the doorway. She pushed them both down to the floor and covered them with her body as a shield. There was so much noise as everything began to crumble around them. Her body took the brunt of the impact.

After seconds of complete terror, everything went silent. All that could be heard was the remnants of debris falling, water spraying out of the broken faucets, and car alarms sounding in the distance.

Alex tried to move but was met with a painful burning sensation to her upper left chest and knew something was wrong. But her first thought was the girls.

"Girls….are you okay?" She asked. She heard them both sniffling, so she knew they were alive.

"Kendra…Kara? Talk to me. I need to hear your voices."

"I'm okay." She heard Kara say.

"Me too." Kendra followed up with.

She tried to move again, but something was sticking in her and preventing her from moving around. She lifted her hand and tried to feel what was around her. There was a lot of debris—concrete chunks, insulation, wires, and glass. She then felt around her chest area under her blazer. When her fingers hit a sharp piece of metal, she realized what had happened and tried not to panic.

"Alex, we need to get out of here," Kendra told her.

"I know, sweetie. The problem is that I'm stuck right now." She took a deep breath, and even that was painful. She wasn't going to tell them that she was impaled. She needed them to stay as calm as possible.

"Oh, god. Alex, there is blood coming from under you," Kendra told Alex, and Alex closed her eyes.

"Kara, reach into my right pocket and pull my phone out."

"Okay. I have it."

"Good, now type in 2team8."

"What kind of password is that?" She asked, and Alex wanted to roll her eyes.

"Focus, Kara."

"Right, sorry."

"It's okay. Are you in?"

"Yes."

"Good, go to my contacts and find the name Tink."

"Got it."

"Call him and tell him where we are and that we need help."

Without being able to see under her, she was worried about how much blood she was losing.

It took several tries to get through, but Kara finally got Tink, and he said he was on his way.

As she laid there, she tried not to move. She needed to reserve all the energy she had left, but she could feel herself starting to fade.

It had felt like an eternity when she finally heard Tink call her name.

"Alex."

"Tink!"

"Alex, is that you?"

"Yes."

"Are Kara and Kendra with you?"

"Yes, they're here, and they're both fine, okay."

She heard concrete being moved, and a few minutes later, Tink appeared above her, and right away, she knew by the expression on his face he understood she was far from alright. She needed to get the girls to safety first because god knew how long it would take to get her out. If she even made it out alive.

"Tink, get the girls out."

"Alex, you need the medical attention."

She pleaded with him. "Tink, please get them out. I don't know how long it will take to get me out."

"Goddammit, Alex."

He attempted to argue with her, but then she lifted her blazer, exposing the metal coming from her chest.

"Oh fuck, baby. We need to get you out first."

"I can't move, Tink. I'm afraid too. It hurts so bad."

"Shit! Hang tight."

He crawled out the hole taking Kendra and Kara with him even though they wanted to stay with her.

When he came back, Mac was with him, and he explained that he had medic training.

"Mind if I take a look?" he asked her.

"Have at it."

As soon as he lifted her blazer, she heard him swear, and that wasn't encouraging.

He then asked her a series of questions. What was the scale of her pain, did she feel faint, nauseous, and other standard questions a doctor would ask.

"I think I'm pretty much fucked, Mac. I'm impaled to the floor."

He gave her a stern look. "Enough of the negative talk."

"We need professionals to get her out," she heard Mac tell Tink.

Then by the grace of God, she heard sirens and prayed they were coming for her.

She took short breaths, trying to calm herself and ease the panic her body was facing. If she wanted any shot of making it out alive, then she needed to relax.

"Dammit, she's really bleeding," Tink said.

Mac ripped his shirt off and stuffed it under her to try and stop as much of the bleeding he could.

"The paramedics are here," Kendra shouted.

"Send them in here," Tink told her.

As two medics made their way in and started to assess her injury, she could tell by their expressions that the outlook wasn't favorable for her.

"Tink?"

"Yeah, sweetie, I'm right here." He pushed her hair from her face, and when she blinked her eyes open, she saw the worry on his face. She couldn't stop the tears from flowing. This isn't how she wanted to go. She was supposed to marry the love of her life in two days. They were supposed to have babies and grow old together. She still had her family and her new family that she hadn't got to know yet. She made a deal with herself that if she survived, she would keep in touch with Kendra and Kara. She couldn't hold them responsible for something their mother did.

"There is so much I want to say right now," she told Tink.

"Alex, don't you dare start talking nonsense right now."

She shook her head. "I don't feel too good."

She squeezed Tink's hand as she tried to focus on him. "I'm scared, Tink."

"Alex, please, sweetie. Don't talk like this."

"This is life, Tink. You of all people should understand."

His watery eyes nearly did her in.

"Alex."

"Tink, please. Promise me that you'll tell my Derek and Ace that I love them."

"No, baby, I'm not going to tell them. You are. Don't give up, Alex. Fight goddamn it!" Tink looked up at Mac, and Mac gave him a grim look.

Another paramedic slid a backboard in, and between the four men, they carefully got her strapped to it on her side.

"She needs a hospital right now. She lost a lot of blood, and her blood pressure is steadily declining."

Tink tried to speak, but he choked on his words.

Just as they started to move her, Alex screamed as a searing pain tore through her body that took her breath away, sending her reeling into what seemed like another world—a world filled with bright white light and silence. It was peaceful.

# CHAPTER NINE

Ace, Derek, Frost, and Stitch rushed into the emergency room and were greeted right away by Tink, who led them through a set of double doors to a private waiting room.

As soon as Tink called and said that Alex was trapped, Derek pulled some strings and got the four of them on a flight out to San Diego.

Ace didn't like the fact that Tink kept quiet. Nor could he take his eyes off the blood staining Tink's shirt.

"Any news since the last update?" Derek asked.

Tink shook his head. "No. She's still in surgery."

As they entered the room, Ace noticed another man standing by the window. As the guy looked up and put away his cell phone, he walked toward them.

"Derek Connors."

"Damn, Mac Ramsey, is that you?"

They hugged and slapped each other on the back.

"What are you doing here?"

"Mac was with me when I got the call about Alex."

"How bad was her injury, Tink?" Stitch asked, looking just as concerned.

Tink shook his head and appeared to bite the inside of his cheek. Ace felt like he wanted to throw up.

"I honestly don't know how she's still alive. All I can say is that it's a fucking miracle. From what the girls told me, Alex threw herself over them to protect them when the ceiling started to collapse. She lost a lot of blood. I don't even know if any organs were damaged. I'm not going to lie to you guys. I'm scared."

Ace swallowed hard.

About another hour went by, the door to the room opened and a doctor wearing scrubs and a nurse entered. Ace could see how tired and drained the

43

doctor appeared and the fact that he wasn't showing any emotion all but told him that he was here to deliver the worst possible news.

"Are you all here for Alexandra Hardesty?" The doctor asked.

Derek stepped forward.

"I'm her dad." Then he pointed to Ace. "And that's her fiancé. The rest are family as well."

The doctor took a deep breath, and Ace braced himself. Nothing could prepare him for the news he was about to receive.

"She's alive."

Ace's head snapped up, and if he wasn't mistaken, every man in that room started to weep.

"I'll be honest with all of you. When she came into the ER, I never expected her to survive, but she fought. I've been practicing medicine in the ER for over twenty years, and I've never seen a miracle play out like I did today." He looked at Derek. "Your daughter had some angels watching over her."

"When will we be able to see her?" Ace asked as he wiped the tears from his eyes.

"Probably in about an hour or two. Once we get her settled, I'll have one of the nurses come and get you."

Ace stepped forward and shook his hand. "Thank you, doctor."

"You hang on to her tight and marry her fast. She's special."

Ace grinned. "I plan to."

As soon as the doctor left the room, all the guys huddled together and hugged each other.

# CHAPTER TEN

A large hand gently caressed Alex's forehead. She stirred a little, wondering why she didn't have much mobility. Her body felt as if it was weighted down. All she could see was darkness. But in the distance, a familiar voice called her name.

"Alex, can you hear me? Come on, sweetheart, show me those beautiful green eyes of yours."

It was a voice she would recognize anywhere. That deep, raspy timbre could only belong to one person.

"Ace?" she whispered.

His large hand cupped her cheek. His touch alone generated a warm sensation deep inside of her that began to spread throughout her body. As the coldness slowly left her body, the darkness impeding her vision began to brighten.

"I'm here, baby," he told her.

She felt as if she was walking toward the light. But it wasn't the light that people spoke about who say they've experienced the afterlife. It was a light to the future.

She stirred again when she felt Ace's warm lips kiss her cheek and then her forehead.

"Come, baby. You're almost there," he cheered as she took those final steps through the light.

She blinked and was blinded by a light above her.

"Shit, hang on, let me turn the light off." She heard Ace say.

He took her hand. "Okay, sweetheart, open those eyes."

She blinked again, then again, before things started coming into focus. Her mouth felt dry, and her body felt numb.

The more she looked around, the fuzziness started to wear off, and then the most beautiful thing came into view.

She smiled. Well, at least she attempted to.

"Hey, sweetheart," Ace said as he leaned down kissed her gently on the lips.

Suddenly, a thought raced into her mind. *Kendra and Kara.*

"The girls." She croaked out. "Are the girls okay?"

Ace took her hand and calmed her. "The girls are fine. They're both safe, thanks to you."

"Oh, good."

She opened her eyes and stared at Ace. "How long have I been asleep?"

"Almost three days."

She processed that. It took a minute for her brain to fire.

"Our wedding. We missed our wedding." She started to cry.

Ace cupped her face in his hands. "Baby, please don't cry. I promise you that as soon as we get home, you and I will get married. The important thing is that you are alive."

There was a knock on the door, and they both turned and saw a nurse. She smiled and walked over to the bed.

"It's great to see you awake," she told Alex.

Alex smiled. "It feels good to be awake."

She handed Alex two pills, and Alex looked at them. "What are these?" She asked.

"Prenatal vitamins that the doctor prescribed."

Alex knew that she wasn't firing on all cylinders, having just awakened, but she could've sworn that the nurse just said prenatal vitamins.

Alex looked at her and tried to hand the pills back. "Ummm...I think you have the wrong patient. I'm not pregnant."

Alex glanced at Ace, and he shook his head as if saying he didn't know what was going on.

She looked back at the nurse, who looked confused. The nurse then rechecked Alex's hospital bracelet.

"This says you're Alexandra Hardesty, and that matches the name on the medicine."

Just then, a doctor entered the room.

He smiled. "I heard someone was awake."

46

Alex smiled. "Finally."

The doctor chuckled then patted her hand. "You're a very lucky young lady."

The nurse looked at the doctor. "Dr. Ingram, there seems to be a mistake with Ms. Hardesty's medication."

The doctor took the paper and the pill bottle from the nurse and looked at them before handing them back to her.

"There's no mistake. That's my signature, and I prescribed those today."

He turned toward Alex. "Did you know that you were pregnant?"

Alex felt as if someone had stuck her with a needle full of caffeine because she was wide awake now.

"I'm sorry. What did you just ask?"

"I asked if you knew that you were pregnant? We ran some blood work today, and your hCG levels came back high."

Alex glanced at Ace, who was still staring at the doctor.

"Are you saying that Alex is pregnant?" Ace asked, and the doctor nodded.

"Congratulations!

Alex swallowed hard. Well, that was a surprise.

The doctor looked her over and told her that her wound was healing nicely and that as long as no infection set in, she could be released in two or three days.

Once he left, Alex looked at Ace. He was still staring at her belly. He hadn't taken his eyes off of it since the doctor gave them the good news. At least she thought it was good news. Ace, on the other hand, started to worry her.

"Ace, are you okay?" She squeezed his hand.

"I'm more than fine," he told her as he raised his head, and the tears in his eyes nearly killed her.

"Ace?"

He leaned over the bed and hugged her, being careful to avoid the side that was injured. She felt the wet tears hit her neck.

"I love you," she whispered to him.

47

He didn't say it back, but his tears of joy told her that she needed to know.

When he pulled back, he kissed her again.

"You really didn't know?" he asked her and shook her head.

"No. I swear."

He smiled. "I'm so fucking happy right now."

"Me too."

He placed his hand over her belly. "I love both of you."

# CHAPTER ELEVEN

It had been a little over a month since the earthquake and Alex's near-death experience. The beginning of her recovery hadn't been all smooth sailings. The day before she was to be discharged from the hospital, she spiked a fever. After multiple blood tests, the doctors had determined that she had developed a serious bacterial infection. But with rigorous antibiotic treatments, she recovered, though not without worry. She and Ace had been afraid that all the trauma she had suffered and all of the medication she needed to recover, it could've impacted their baby's health. When she brought up her concerns to her doctors, they all assured her that everything appeared fine with the baby.

After being permitted by her doctors to travel, she and Ace had snuck off to the Caribbean to enjoy a few days together in peace. It was the honeymoon destination that Ace had chosen to surprise her with, even though they still weren't married.

Both Ace and she loved their family and friends dearly and knew they only had good intentions, but their front door had been a continuous revolving door of visitors since she returned home.

Everyone had been delighted when she and Ace announced they were expecting. Alex thought that Derek was more thrilled than anyone. Of course, having a baby brought the question of when were they going to get married. Their response was "when it happened." Until then, they were enjoying the time of being together because they both knew that was all that mattered.

As she lay in bed listening to the ocean waves gently lap the shoreline, she kept thinking about angels. It was strange, but ever since she had woken up in the hospital every night, she had been visited by an angel in her dreams. She never could see the face, but the presence in the dreams always seemed to comfort her.

49

She felt those strong muscled arms wrap around her, and she smiled as Ace's lips pressed along her shoulder and his large hand covered her belly, which was starting to show.

She looked over her shoulder and gazed into those blue eyes, and she felt like she fell in love all over again.

"Hey, sweetheart."

She smiled. "Hi." She rolled over and laid her head on his shoulder.

"What's on your mind? You've got that I'm thinking look." He asked, rubbing the spot between her eyes.

"Do you believe in angels?"

Ace squinted his eyes then caressed her cheek.

"I do," he answered as he stared deep into her eyes.

"You do?"

He nodded his head. "I'm looking at one right now."

"Ace, I'm serious."

"I am too. Many people I've met throughout my life may not wear halos or have white wings, but it's their actions that convince me that angels truly do walk amongst us here on earth."

"Why did you ask?"

She never told him about her dreams. "Ever since I was in the hospital, every night I've dreamt of an angel visiting me, but I never see his or face."

Ace caressed her cheek. "Maybe it's angels giving you your wings and halo because you have earned them."

"Maybe." She said and curled into his side.

"Would you be okay by yourself for a bit?"

She scrunched her nose up. "Where are you going?"

"I need to run over to the business center. Derek sent a text telling me that I needed to check my email. And you know that the internet connection isn't strong here in the room."

He wasn't exaggerating. The connection sucked.

She frowned and sat up. "Do you think we have to leave?" She would be devastated if they had to leave the island.

"I don't think so. But I'll be back shortly because I promised you a romantic night on the beach."

She smiled. "I've been looking forward to it since you mentioned it."

Before he got out of bed, he handed her an envelope. "Don't open this until after I leave."

She gave him a curious look, wondering what he was up to. But she agreed. They had stayed in bed all day just talking and napping.

He dressed then kissed her and her belly before he left.

Once she knew he was gone, she sat up and leaned against the headboard. She slipped her finger under the envelope seal and pulled out a small piece of paper.

Written in his handwriting were the words, *I brought an outfit for you to wear to our dinner tonight. It's in the closet.*

She grinned and got herself out of bed and walked to the closet. She was a little nervous because this was totally out of character for Ace. He never picked out her clothes.

When she turned the knob and pulled the door open, she gasped, and the tears burned her eyes. Hanging in the center of the closet like a window dressing was her wedding dress with a note attached to it that read, *I promised that you would get your happily ever after. At five o'clock there will be a knock on the door. Go with them and follow the trail of lights.*

Her hands were shaking as she reached for the dress. As she wiped the tears from her eyes, she looked at the clock. She only had forty-five minutes to get ready.

At five o'clock sharp, there was a knock at the door. She was a little nervous that a stranger was coming to take her to her wedding. But when she opened the door, the eight men standing before in their Navy Dress Whites were anything but strangers.

"Oh, my, God!" She sobbed at the sight of all her uncles. Derek held out his hand and smiled. "You look absolutely beautiful. We are here to escort you to your wedding."

She looped her arm with Derek's, and they walked the lighted path that took them down to the beach. As they approached a large fountain, Derek stopped her. Without saying a word, he handed her a letter envelope. It looked old and worn, and she looked at Derek for him to explain.

Through tears in his eyes, he told her, "Your dad wanted you to have that on your wedding day."

She looked at the envelope then back at Derek. "Do I read it now?"

He softly smiled. "I think he'd want you to."

Alex walked over to the fountain and sat on the ledge.

She held her breath as she opened the envelope and pulled out the piece of paper. She closed her eyes and took a deep breath. Once she felt she had collected herself, she opened her eyes and began to read.

*Dear Alex,*

*Since the day you came into this world, you have been my heart and soul. You were the ray of sunshine that helped me through some of my darkest days. You were the little girl that I swore I was never going to let grow up.*

*But if you're reading this, it means you have blossomed into a woman who is moments away from sharing a life of happiness and love with the man that you've given your heart to.*

*It pains me not to be there to walk you down the aisle, but know I'm walking with you in spirit as you march toward your future.*

*I will be watching from above as you pledge your heart and devotion to the man you love.*

*And know that I will always be that angel watching over you and your family.*

*Always and forever,*
*Dad*

Alex tried her best to blink back the tears, but it was tough. She never knew that her dad had written that letter, but it didn't surprise her either. It gave her peace to know he was there.

She heard footsteps approaching and looked up and met Derek's gaze. She folded up the letter and tucked it into her bouquet.

"You ready?" Derek asked

"I am," she whispered low. She could hardly speak because of the emotion she was feeling on the inside.

As she and Derek walked arm and arm, she heard the music begin to play, and she felt her body fill with excitement, knowing that in less than twenty minutes or so, she would become Mrs. Marcus Chambers.

As she rounded the final bend expecting to find her husband to be waiting for her, she was dealt another surprise that had her crying once more. Not only were all of their friends and family there, but Ace had managed to have the beach decorated with everything she had wanted for their wedding.

As another song began to play, Derek glanced at her. "You ready, honey?"

She gave him a teary-eyed, cheeky grin. "Ready as I'll ever be."

As Alex started down the aisle, she met Ace's gaze. Seeing the tears in his eyes nearly brought her to her knees. He looked so handsome in dress whites. As they made it to the alter, Derek kissed her cheek before handing her off to Ace.

Ace took her and hand and brought it to his lips.

"Are you okay?" he asked.

She gave him the biggest smile she could muster.

"I'm more than okay. I'm marrying the man I love while my angel watches from above."

They both smiled and glanced down at the seat on the end they had reserved for her dad.

Ace bent down and kissed her cheek.

"I love you."

"I love you too, Ace, and I always will."

# BOOK LIST

## The Trident Series

ACE
POTTER
FROST
IRISH
STITCH
DINO
SKITTLES
DIEGO *(2021)*
A TRIDENT WEDDING *(2021)*

## The Trident Series II
## BRAVO Team

JOKER *(2021)*
BEAR *(2022)*
DUKE *(2022)*
PLAYBOY *(2022)*
AUSSIE *(2022)*
SNOW *(2022)*
NAILS *(TBD)*
JAY BIRD *(TBD)*

# ABOUT THE AUTHOR

Jaime Lewis, a *USA TODAY* bestselling author, entered the indie author world in June 2020 with ACE, the first book in the Trident Series.

With a barrage of positive reviews and a series embraced by readers, Jaime is a rising star in the romantic suspense genre.

Coming from a military family, she describes as very patriotic; it's no surprise that her books are known for their accurate portrayal of life in the service.

Passionate in her support of the military, veterans, and first responders, Jaime volunteers with the Daytona Division of the US Naval Sea Cadet Corps, a non-profit youth leadership development program sponsored by the U.S. Navy. Together with her son, she also manages a charity organization that supports military personnel and their families, along with veterans and first responders.

Born and raised in Edgewater, Maryland, Jaime now resides in Ormond Beach, Florida with her husband and two very active boys.

Between her day job, her two boys, and writing, she doesn't have a heap of spare time, but if she does, you'll find her somewhere in the outdoors. Jaime is also an avid sports fan.

Follow Jaime:

Facebook Author Page:https://www.facebook.com/jaime.lewis.58152
Jaime's Convoy: https://www.facebook.com/groups/349178512953776
Goodreads: https://www.goodreads.com/author/show/17048191.Jaime_Lewis

Made in the USA
Las Vegas, NV
06 October 2021

31803700R00037